# THE TWELVE DAYS OF
# CHRISTMAS

In memory of my father, Don

Copyright © 2011 by Jane Ray

First U.S. edition 2011

First published in Great Britain in 2011 by Orchard Books

Library of Congress Cataloging-in-Publication Data

Ray, Jane.
The twelve days of Christmas / Jane Ray. — 1st U.S. ed.
p.   cm.
Summary: On each of the twelve days of Christmas,
more and more gifts arrive from the recipient's true love.
ISBN 978-0-7636-5735-2
1. Folk songs, English — England — Texts. 2. Christmas music — Texts.
[1. Folk songs — England.  2. Christmas music.]   I. Title.
PZ8.3.R2331Tw  2011
782.42'17230268 — dc22       2010052222

11 12 13 14 15 16 WKT 10 9 8 7 6 5 4 3 2 1

Printed in Shenzhen, Guangdong, China

This book was typeset in Fairfield LH.
The illustrations were done in mixed media.

Candlewick Press
99 Dover Street
Somerville, Massachusetts 02144

visit us at www.candlewick.com

# THE TWELVE DAYS OF CHRISTMAS

To
My True Love
x

## Jane Ray

CANDLEWICK PRESS

On the first day of Christmas,
my true love sent to me
a partridge in a pear tree.

On the second day of Christmas,
  my true love sent to me:
two turtledoves
and a partridge in a pear tree.

On the third day of Christmas,
my true love sent to me:
three French hens,
two turtledoves,
and a partridge in a pear tree.

On the fourth day of Christmas,
   my true love sent to me:
four calling birds,
three French hens,
two turtledoves,
and a partridge in a pear tree.

On the fifth day of Christmas,
   my true love sent to me:
five golden rings . . .

four calling birds,
three French hens,
two turtledoves,
and a partridge in a pear tree.

On the sixth day of Christmas,
  my true love sent to me:
six geese a-laying,
five golden rings,
four calling birds,
three French hens,
two turtledoves,
and a partridge in a pear tree.

On the seventh day of Christmas,
  my true love sent to me:
seven swans a-swimming,
six geese a-laying,
five golden rings,
four calling birds,
three French hens,
two turtledoves,
and a partridge in a pear tree.

On the eighth day of Christmas,
   my true love sent to me:
eight maids a-milking,
seven swans a-swimming,
six geese a-laying,
five golden rings,
four calling birds,
three French hens,
two turtledoves,
and a partridge in a pear tree.

On the ninth day of Christmas,
    my true love sent to me:
nine ladies dancing,
eight maids a-milking,
seven swans a-swimming,
six geese a-laying,
five golden rings,
four calling birds,
three French hens,
two turtledoves,
and a partridge in a pear tree.

On the tenth day of Christmas,
  my true love sent to me:
ten lords a-leaping,
nine ladies dancing,
eight maids a-milking,
seven swans a-swimming,

six geese a-laying,
five golden rings,
four calling birds,
three French hens,
two turtledoves,
and a partridge in a pear tree.

On the eleventh day of Christmas,
    my true love sent to me:
eleven pipers piping,
ten lords a-leaping,
nine ladies dancing,
eight maids a-milking,
seven swans a-swimming,

six geese a-laying,
five golden rings,
four calling birds,
three French hens,
two turtledoves,
and a partridge in a pear tree.

On the twelfth day of Christmas,
  my true love sent to me:
twelve drummers drumming,
eleven pipers piping,
ten lords a-leaping,
nine ladies dancing . . .

eight maids a-milking,
seven swans a-swimming,
six geese a-laying,
five golden rings,
four calling birds,
three French hens,
two turtledoves . . .

and a partridge in a pear tree.